To Mrs. Cade,
May you enjoy and appreciate this
historical fiction.

Best Wishes!
S. Marie
1-12-90

Tears For Ashan

by D. Marie

Illustrations by Norman Childers

Creative Press Works

Memphis, Tennessee

Printed in the U.S.A.

Creative Press Works
P. O. Box 280556
Memphis, Tennessee

Copyright 1988 by D. Marie

Library of Congress Cataloging-in-Publication Data

Marie, D., 1954—
    Tears for Ashan.

    Summary: A young African boy's friendship with an older boy ends when the latter is taken away on a slave ship.

[1. Slavery–Fiction. 2. Africa–Fiction]
I. Childers, Norman H., 1953— ill. II. Title.
PZ7.M33838Te 1989   [E]   88-63766
ISBN 0-9621681-0-6

Library of Congress Card Number: 88-63766

ISBN: 0-9621681-0-6

Typography and printing by Desktop Publishers of Memphis.

This book is for my children, April, James, and Maya
whose curiosity extends beyond the limited dimensions of television.

Special thanks to

Dr. Juanita Williamson, Chairman
Literature Department at Lemoyne Owens College, Memphis, TN

Cary Jehl & Associates, Public Relations Consultants
James E. Carter, M. D.
Marilyn D. Carter, Ph.D., Ed.

Foreword to Parents

This book is for caring, inquisitive children and parents who have the wisdom and foresight to help their children begin to understand a subject seldom discussed with young children —slavery. Except for here, you will not see the term again.

It is hoped that the story itself, as seen through the eyes of a young boy, will provide children with some understanding and appreciation of life as it must have been before the big ships came. Your children, as mine, and many of their friends, will want to know what happened to Ashan. For now, you must answer that question for them. You must begin to help them understand an unpleasant historical fact. For it is through their awareness and appreciation of history that they develop a respect for all people.

Long, long ago, in
a land called Africa,
there once lived a
boy named Kumasi.
Kumasi, and the other
members of his family, lived in a little hut near the ocean.

Kumasi, like the other boys in his village, spent most of his time hunting or fishing. At the end of the day, many of the boys entertained themselves with friendly wrestling matches.

When he was not out hunting or playing, Kumasi could be found studying with the wise man of his village. Here, he would learn the history of his people as well as their customs.

When study time was over, Kumasi would rush over to visit Ashan. Although Ashan was much older than Kumasi, he was Kumasi's best friend!

Ashan had taught Kumasi many things. He taught him
how to look and listen for signs of danger in the forest.

It was Ashan who had shown him how to use the bark of the trees to paint his face to look like a fierce warrior.

Today,
Ashan would show him
how to throw his spear so it
would go further than any of the spears thrown
by the other boys in their village.

   Those boys, who had learned the ways of the forest,
were allowed to go along on hunting trips with the men
of the village. Kumasi felt very proud when he walked
alongside his father and the other men as they
prepared to leave on a hunting trip.

One day,
while they were
on a hunting trip,
the group spotted a ship that was anchored offshore. As they
hid behind the bushes, they watched as some men left the
big ship for a smaller one. They were led ashore by someone
who looked as if he may have come from a nearby tribe.

   As they came on shore,
these men appeared quite strange to Kumasi: Although
they were men like his father, their hair was straight,
and their skin was without color!

They carried heavy chains.

In the place of arrows or spears, they had long sticks that smoked and made a loud popping noise.

Kumasi's father spoke to the others, "We must go back and warn the others. It is now time to move our village." He continued, "The drums sent a message to beware of these strangers, who take people away from their village.

"Those taken are put on the big ship and taken to a far away land where they are never heard of again."

When they returned to the village,
Kumasi's father hurried to tell
the chief all that he had seen.

Soon the entire village
was busy with people
preparing for the move. Kumasi and Ashan ran off
to help their families prepare for the move.

The tribe was ready to move at dawn. They were sad. They had to leave many of their special things behind.

Suddenly, there were popping sounds all around them. The strangers had found their village!

Women and children ran to the forest for safety.

The men grabbed for weapons to defend their village.
Ashan's and Kumasi's fathers joined the others. In the confusion,
Kumasi was separated from his family. He climbed up a tall tree in
the forest and watched the fight below. He knew he would be safe.

The men from the village fought bravely
but their spears were no match for the weapons
the strangers carried. They were frightened by the popping sounds
that came from these strange weapons.
All who were quick enough escaped into the forest.

Kumasi's father was able to escape,
but Ashan was not. Kumasi saw him being
taken by the strangers. He decided he would follow.
He could not leave Ashan in the hands of these strangers,
and there was not enough time to get help from his father.
He would be careful to remain hidden by the forest. When the
time was right, he thought to himself, he would help Ashan escape.

It was almost dark when the strangers made it back to thei
ship. It had been a long journey for Kumasi to make alone.
He was tired, and his legs were covered with scratches from
the thickets in the forest. To soothe his pain, he made a
dressing from the leaves of certain plants in the forest.

From his place in the bush,
he watched as one of the strangers held Ashan, while
another put a chain around his ankle. Watching this
made him very sad, because he knew Ashan would not be
able to run away from these strangers. Kumasi
also knew his plans to help Ashan escape were doomed.

Kumasi spent the night on the beach. The next morning, he sadly watched as Ashan and the others were given bread and water. Afterwards, they were taken away to the big ship.

Kumasi wept
because he knew he would never see Ashan again.

About the author . . .

D. Marie is a Louisiana native, who presently resides in Memphis, Tennessee. She holds a degree in history from Northeast Louisiana University; she attended Loyola University, School of Law, where she earned a doctorate in jurisprudence. She is a licensed attorney and the mother of three children, ages 2–7. In addition to writing, she continues to pursue a legal career.

About the illustrator . . .

Norman Childers, also known as "Pouncho", is a self-taught artist and illustrator, who lives in Memphis, Tennessee. He has authored and illustrated his own work entitled, "The Great Monkey Debate", published by White Rose Press.